W9-ATB-835

rabbit ears

Text copyright © 2006 by Amber Stewart
Illustrations copyright © 2006 by Laura Rankin
All rights reserved. No part of this book may be used or reproduced
in any manner whatsoever without written permission from the publisher,
except in the case of brief quotations embodied in critical articles or reviews.

Typeset in Cheltenham Light
The art was created with acrylic inks and paints on Arches watercolor paper
Design by Filomena Tuosto

Published by Bloomsbury Publishing, New York, London, and Berlin
Distributed to the trade by Holtzbrinck Publishers

Library of Congress Cataloging-in-Publication Data
Stewart, Amber.
Rabbit ears / Amber Stewart ; illustrated by Laura Rankin.
p. cm.
Summary: Hopscotch the rabbit refuses to wash his ears until his
older cousin comes to visit and he learns something about being grown up.
ISBN-10: 1-58234-959-2 • ISBN-13: 978-1-58234-959-6
[1. Baths—Fiction. 2. Ear—Fiction. 3. Cleanliness—Fiction. 4. Rabbits—Fiction.]
I. Rankin, Laura, ill. II. Title.
PZ7.S84868Rab 2006 [E]—dc22 2005054578

First U.S. Edition 2006
Printed in China
1 3 5 7 9 10 8 6 4 2

Bloomsbury Publishing, Children's Books, U.S.A.
175 Fifth Avenue, New York, NY 10010

All papers used by Bloomsbury Publishing are natural, recyclable products
made from wood grown in well-managed forests. The manufacturing processes
conform to the environmental regulations of the country of origin.

rabbit ears

Amber Stewart

illustrated by Laura Rankin

To my very lovely Lottie and Josh
I love you — clean ears or not
— A.S.

For Tyler and Ryan
— L.R.

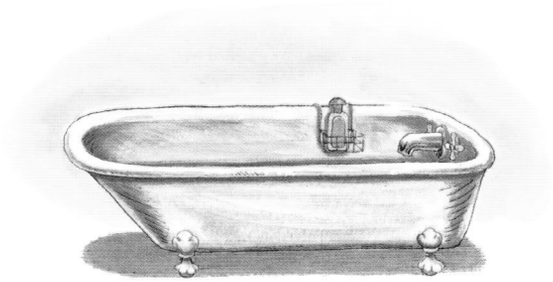

Hopscotch knew what he liked and what he did not like.

He did like Rabbity,

building a tower
twelve blocks high
with no wobbles at all,

and very chocolaty chocolate cake
(with extra icing on the side).

Hopscotch did not like
lumpy pudding,

cold wet paws,

and losing Rabbity just before bedtime, even though Rabbity
was usually found exactly where Hopscotch had left him.

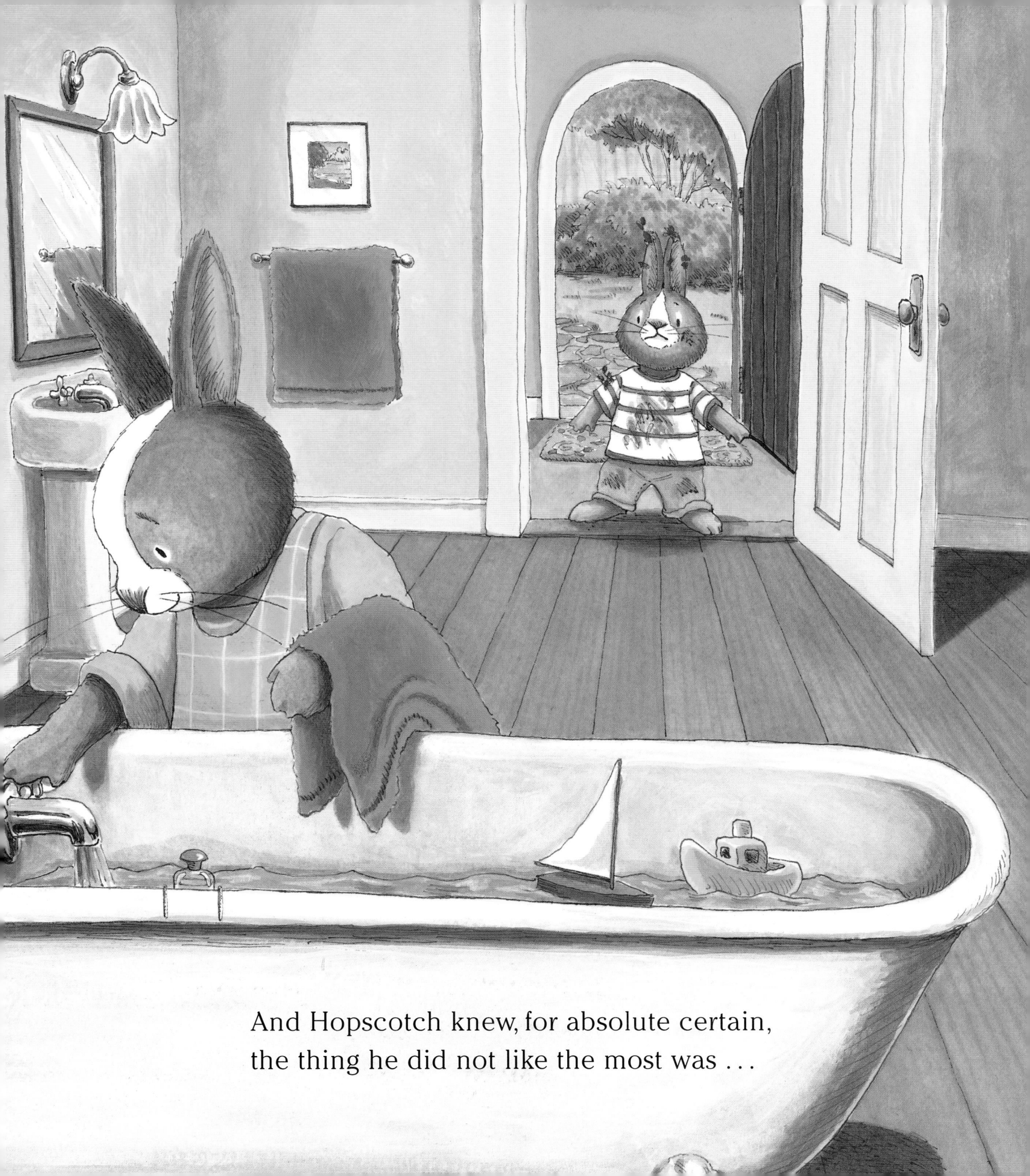

And Hopscotch knew, for absolute certain,
the thing he did not like the most was . . .

. . . having his ears washed!

Hopscotch liked his ears dry.
He did not like them soapy.
The soap always ran away, then ended up
in his nose and made him sneeze.
The sneezes shook him from
his soggy, drippy ears to his toes.
Hopscotch didn't like it one little bit.

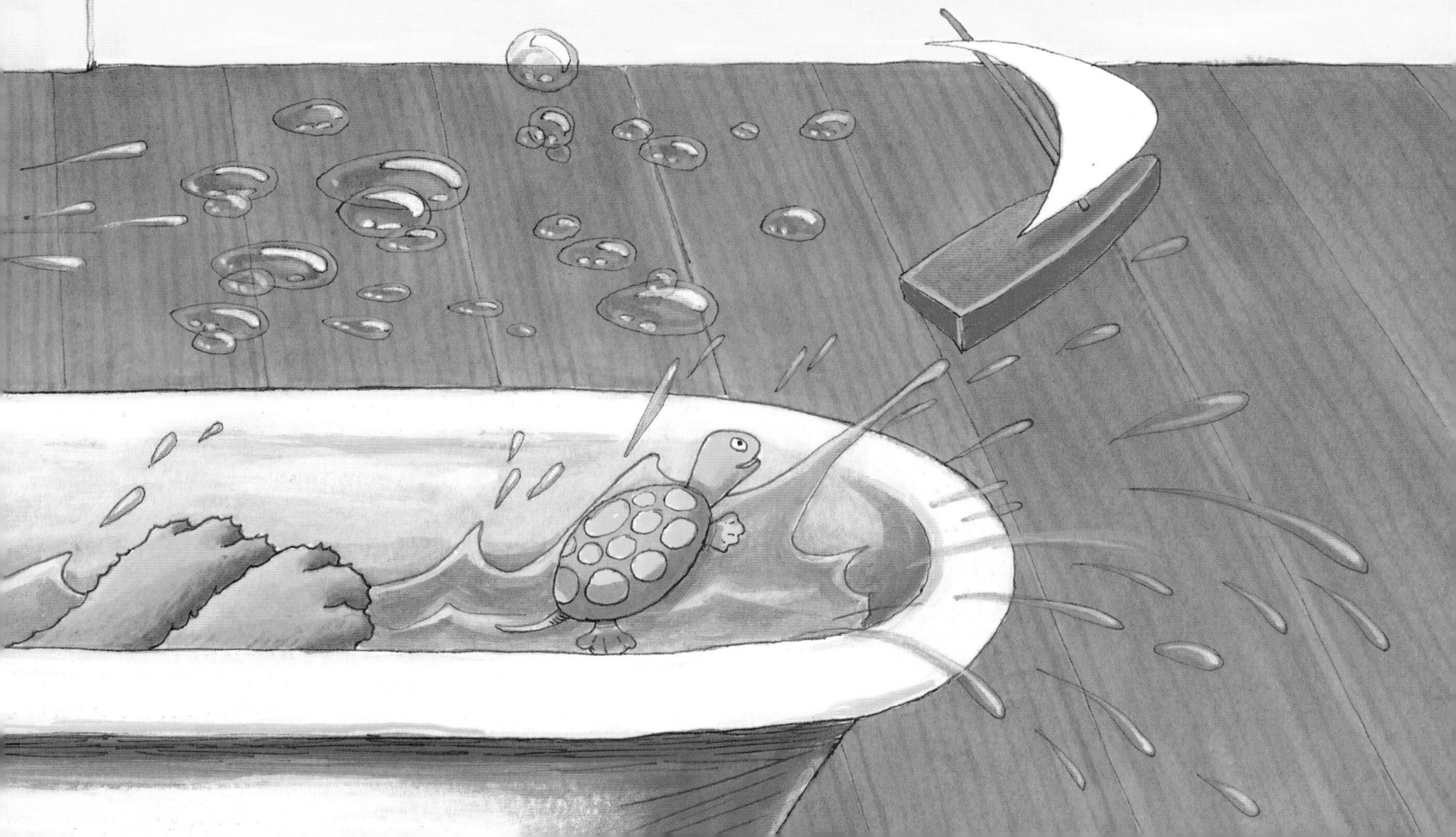

Hopscotch would do a lot not to have his ears washed.

With Rabbity's help, he would hide them.

Sometimes he'd pretend that he had suddenly turned into a cat—a cat with very small, clean ears.

Or he would hold on to them very, very tightly.

Hopscotch's mother tried tricking him . . .
"Where's the airplane?"

Hopscotch's mother tried begging him . . .
"Please, just this once?"

She even tried chocolate cake . . .
"Look, it's your favorite."
But nothing worked.

One day, Hopscotch's big cousin Bobtail
came to stay—just for one day and a night.

Hopscotch and Bobtail played high jump, long jump.

Then they listened for danger as they rescued Rabbity from the lion's den.

They played and played until all too soon it was suppertime.

"When can I go and stay all by myself at Bobtail's?" asked Hopscotch through a mouthful of extra-chocolaty chocolate cake.

"When you are big, little Hopscotch," said Daddy.
"When you are big." After supper, it was time for a bath.

Hopscotch was happily playing submarines
when he noticed something odd . . .

Bobtail was washing his own ears!
He didn't seem to mind the runaway soap.
Not one bit.
And he didn't get the sneezes at all.
Not one sneeze.

"Big rabbits wash their own ears," thought Hopscotch.

Hopscotch felt it might be a good idea
to practice ear-washing on Rabbity first.
Rabbity didn't seem to mind it at all—
in fact, they had fun with all the bubbles.

"What are you up to, Hopscotch?" asked Daddy.
"I'm practicing," said Hopscotch.
"Practicing what?" asked Daddy.
"Practicing washing my ears so I can be big and go and stay with Bobtail all by myself," said Hopscotch.
"Well," said Daddy, "that's wonderful!"

Hopscotch knew what he liked and what he *really* liked.
He liked bathtime with Rabbity and clean soapy ears.

He *really* liked singing a song with Mommy
to celebrate his very clean ears.

Soapy, soapy, soapy ears, soapy ears,
soapy ears
Washy, washy, washy ears, washy ears,
washy ears
Fluffy, fluffy, fluffy ears, fluffy ears,
fluffy ears
All day long!

And best of all, he liked
packing his favorite games,

waving good-bye to Mommy and Daddy,

and going to stay with big cousin Bobtail for one whole day and a night all by himself. Well, almost . . .

Rabbity came too.